Other books in the series:

The Adventures of Chee and Dae in Ishcra-Bochra

The Adventures of Chee and Dae in Droskeen

Illustrated by Mashal Irfan

Secondary Illustrations: Arifa Sayla

Creative Editor: Kieren Knapp

First Edition 2018

Published by: The Wadi Tribe Publishing House

© Copyright Protected by the author

This book is dedicated to my Dad for enriching my life with endless magical stories. To my children Alizeh & Zain, for their encouragement & support.

To Breandan Mac Sitric for co-creating Chee and Dae. A gentleman and a great human being.

To Mashal and Hira for making this book a reality. I shall always treasure the laughs we shared through the creative process.

Finally, I dedicate this book to all those who love mystery, magic and adventure!

Contents Page

Chapter 1

The Hawa Cave

Chee was a bright little chimpanzee born in a mystical land full of great places and stories. He was a very curious chimp and at times got into a lot of trouble because of it.

However, he was always very helpful and caring. Even when he was being naughty, Chee could never hurt anyone's feelings and always made sure he cleaned up whatever mess he made.

Usually, he got into trouble on account of his curiosity. Often he would try to find a hiding place when he was going to be punished. One day, he found one such place only by accident. And oh, what a beautiful magical place it was, where all his dreams came true! More importantly, that is also where he met his best friend, Dae the dolphin.

Let me explain how it all started.

Chee the chimpanzee was outside, playing football with his friends. He may have been just a small monkey, but today he was more like an excitable kangaroo, bouncing and springing about the place!

Chee was often so busy having fun that he would sometimes forget about the world around him. And that's exactly what happened to him this time! He'd kept on playing football long after his friends had gone home. It wasn't until the first drops of rain fell that he realised he was on his own.

Oh, no! Mum's going to be so worried! Chee thought to himself. He picked up his gear and started to run towards home. It was getting dark and he had a long way to go.

"I'm in trouble already, so I must run faster, faster!" Chee said with a smile; he loved running, and feeling the wind and drizzle on his

3

face was so much fun.

Chee was running along a narrow cliff edge. The soil was weak and slippery underfoot. He should have been more careful, but he was so excited. He trod in a patch of wet soil; his leg gave way, and he went tumbling.

Chee flailed his arms wildly in the air, trying to grab hold of anything to stop his fall. But it was no use; the rain had made everything too slippery. So down he rolled, eventually hitting what looked like a muddy slide through a long, dark tunnel.

Whiiiiiiiiishhh!

It seemed like a very long time to Chee before he finally landed on something big and soft. He looked down and sniffed at it. "Phew! It's squishy moss!" he said, heaving a sigh of relief. "Thank goodness, I could have been hurt very badly."

Chee brushed the muck off his fur and checked to see if anything was broken. Apart from a few scratches here and there, he seemed to be alright.

Chee looked around the place to see where he was. It appeared to be a cave, surrounded with old trees. It was dark now, but the stars were shining brightly against a full moon, and a star sparkled close to it. As his eyes adjusted, Chee saw through the branches that there was water outside. He could smell the salty sea and hear soft waves.

"Perfect! I can clean the rest of my fur in the salt water," Chee said, before running towards the water.

He took a few steps towards the water, but then stopped for a moment. "Wow! What a beautiful place!"

It was magical! The moon was reflecting off the surface of the water and each wave softly disappeared into a white sandy beach. It looked like a little estuary hidden away from the world, with trees and rocks and stones, all bathed in the moonlight.

Chee had never seen such natural beauty before. He stood there for a few moments taking it all in, awestruck. A grin spread across his face; he had such a sense of peace and calm here.

"Hmmm, I feel so happy and content here. It must be magical. It must be."

Chee looked down at the white sand and suddenly realised that drops of blood from one of his scratches had fallen on the white beach.

"Oops! Better get this cleaned first."

Chee skipped to the water and gently put his hand in it. The water was soothingly warm and he couldn't resist playing for a few minutes. Gone was any thought about his mum and home. He kicked off his football boots and dug his feet in the wet sand; it felt like paradise.

Chee wasn't sure how long he had been sitting there when a soft ripple in the water nearby startled him. He jumped up and strained his eyes towards the middle of the estuary to see what had made the noise. At first he couldn't see anything, but then he saw a long shape just below the surface. It looked so

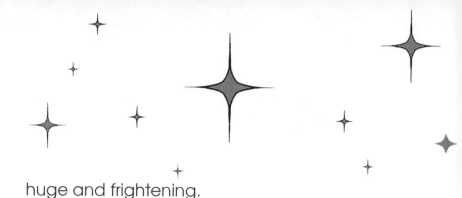

huge and frightening.

Chee stood frozen in fear, staring at the shadow in the water. Then suddenly, the large shadow jumped out and landed with a big splash near him. Chee screamed and shut his eyes tightly. When he heard giggles, he slowly opened them.

There was a strange creature staring back at Chee, its head partially submerged. Only its eyes showed above the water; they were wide and beautiful.

Chee relaxed, sensing that the strange creature meant him no harm. But just as he went to introduce himself, the creature once again disappeared beneath the surface, before jumping out again and crashing back down, drenching Chee in a wave of water!

The creature stared Chee in the eye,

whistled loudly and finally spoke: "Hey! You are in my secret place!"

"Aaa ... ooo hmmmm," Chee muttered back.

The creature giggled. "Boo!"

Chee jumped, sending the creature into more fits of laughter.

"Sorry, I didn't mean to scare you. I got startled when I saw you at Fizz."

The creature spoke with a softly sweet voice that Chee felt drawn to.

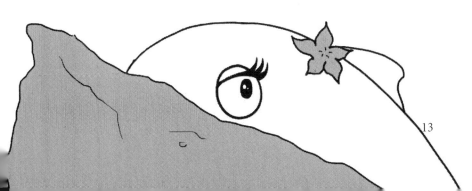

"Fizz?" Chee asked.

"This is my secret relaxation spot. I call it Fizz. Strange, I thought no one else knew of it!"

"I was running home when I slipped and fell," Chee explained. "This is where I ended up."

"Yes," she said, jumping out of the water again and splashing Chee.

"Hey!" Chee shrieked. "Stop it!"

The creature giggled again and looked at Chee with a naughty look. "Sorry, couldn't help myself."

"You're not sorry at all," Chee said, shaking the water off him, but he couldn't help but smile.

The creature pushed itself onto a flat rock, close to the beach. It was then that Chee realised what it was: a dolphin! He had never seen one before. He couldn't help but like her; she had such a beautiful and kind face.

"Hi, I'm Dae!" said the dolphin, reaching out a flipper towards Chee. Chee shook her flipper and introduced himself.

"Cheeeeee...that's a very funny name!" Dae smiled. "Is it short for something?"

"No," Chee said, smiling sheepishly. "My mum thought I looked like a Chee when I was born."

Dae laughed heartily. "I like your name – it suits you," she said.

"Does 'Dae' have a meaning?" Chee asked.

"Yes, it means freedom, in the magical world!" Dae giggled and splashed Chee with her tail.

"Hey! Stop that!"

"OK, sorry – again!" Dae said with a shy grin. She jumped off the rock and swam closer to the shore. "I didn't know this cave had another entrance; where did you come in Chee?"

Chee moved a large branch at the back of the cave, revealing a hole. "There's a natural mud slide in there that I slid down through; I think it might be a blowhole made by the sea."

17

"Wow! That slide sounds like a lot of fun. Where does it start?" Dae asked.

"There's a patch near the football pitch, hidden under the old mulberry bush," Chee explained. "I guess the rain opened it up. I slipped and I slid down and down, and I ended up here in this cave!"

"The Hawa cave," Dae smiled.

"The Hawa cave?" Chee asked.

"Yes, 'Hawa' means 'wind' in many languages." Dae's eyes lit up. "If you listen carefully, you can hear the wind sing. Sometimes you can even hear the messages other winds bring."

"Wow!" Chee ran towards the Hawa cave, plopped himself down on the large rock and tilted his head, trying to hear the Hawa.

"But, I can't hear anything," he muttered.

"Shhh," Dae said. "Close your eyes, sit perfectly still, and listen."

Chee smirked; he didn't have the patience to sit still and listen! But there was something in Dae's voice, a calmness, that relaxed him. He closed his eyes.

A minute passed, and then another. Then suddenly, Chee heard a gentle 'swish' as cool air poured into the cave. It blew gently and encircled him. Chee was frightened, yet excited at the same time. He opened his eyes to see a trail of soft blue mist all around him, like millions of glowing blue particles. It was pure magic.

Dae watched with a smile as Chee's eyes widened in fascination. The blue wind had now spread all around the cave. Suddenly, the wind whispered gently into Chee's ear: "Centipede."

Chee shrieked and jumped atop a rock as the magical wind disappeared and the cave fell into pin-drop silence.

"What's wrong?" asked Dae. "What did the wind say to you?"

"Ce-ce-centipede!" Chee replied, frantically looking around for the creepy-crawly. He didn't like bugs, least of all centipedes.

"Eeeeeee!" screamed Dae, jumping up and down.

Chee was still trying to understand what was going on, and now Dae was jumping in and out of the water, splashing water all over him.

"What is it Dae?" Chee asked, shaking the water off him again.

"Don't worry Chee! It's not a creepy-crawly centipede!"

Chee relaxed as his new friend smiled at him. "It's a train!" she said.

★

Chapter 2
The CP Train

The next day, Chee ran towards Fizz, found the wet patch and slid through the tunnel into the cave.

Dae was waiting for him, jumping in and out of the water. "Looks like you ran all the way here!" she said, smiling as always.

"Yes, I had all my chores finished in an hour. Mum was so surprised. Is the CP Train here yet?"

Dae had told Chee all about the magical train that passed through the cave. It was called the Centipede Train, but as Chee disliked centipedes so much, even their name, they'd both agreed to call it the CP Train.

"The train will be here soon. Come on, jump on my back; we have to go to the rock on the other side of the estuary," Dae said.

Chee looked at her hesitantly. He was a bit nervous to jump on Dae's back, but at the same time he didn't want to miss the train. He closed his eyes and gently climbed onto her back.

"Hang on tight to my dorsal fin," she said, and as soon as Chee did, she zoomed towards the rock with a whishhh!

"Yeee!" Chee exclaimed, full of nervous excitement.

Dae stopped by the rock, which was larger than it looked and flat at the top.

"This is the train platform," Dae explained. "If you listen carefully, you'll hear the train approaching."

Chee listened for the train. It wasn't long before he heard it: Chugga-chugga-chug-

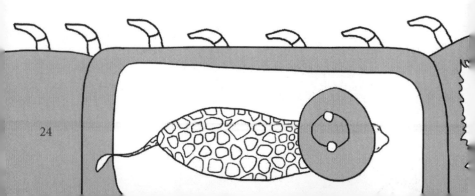

24

25

ga chugga-chugga-chugga chugga-chug-ga-chugga!

Chee gasped as the train suddenly appeared out of nowhere. "The train looks like a large centipede!" he exclaimed, terrified.

"Don't be scared Chee!" Dae said, reassuring her frightened friend. "We have to be quick; it slows down only for a few seconds in Fizz."

Dae arched her back, pushing Chee down towards her tail, before flicking him towards the train!

Chee landed with a bump in a box filled with straw. Dae jumped into the box filled with water behind him. The water splashed all over Chee – again!

Dae laughed at poor, drenched Chee. "Oops, sorry."

Chee looked around. The CP Train seemed to have millions of tiny legs, which flitted through small grooves in the ground.

"Look, it's Zarfe, the giraffe from Zanzibar!" Dae said when she caught Chee looking at a long necked animal in the box behind her. "Zanzibar is a beautiful place in Africa."

Chee couldn't help but stare at Zarfe; he'd never seen a giraffe before. Zarfe met his gaze for a second, before looking away.

"Zarfe is a bit shy," Dae said. "She gets very nervous when you stare at her."

Chee quickly looked away. "Are there many places outside Fizz?" he asked, changing the subject.

"Oh, yes, so many." Dae smiled. "We can travel to all of them!"

Chee grinned. "The adventures of Chee and Dae!" he declared excitedly.

"Yippee!" Dae shouted, and the two of them smiled, looking forward to all the adventures to come.

Suddenly they heard, "Aah, hot! Ooh, hot! Aah, hot!" It was coming from the box in front of Chee.

Chee and Dae leaned over to see a desert lizard hopping on all its feet, screaming, "Aah, hot! Ooh, hot! Aah, hot!"

"What's wrong?" Chee asked.

"My feet are burning on this hot sand!" the lizard said, its eyes rolling around.

"But you're a desert lizard – aren't you supposed to handle heat?" Dae asked.

"Aah, hot! Ooh, hot! I wasn't born with those kind of feet. Aaaaah! Please help!"

"Quick! Jump in my box – it has straw in it."

The lizard threw itself in Chee's box. It was so big and clumsy.

"Quick! Lift your feet!" Dae said to the

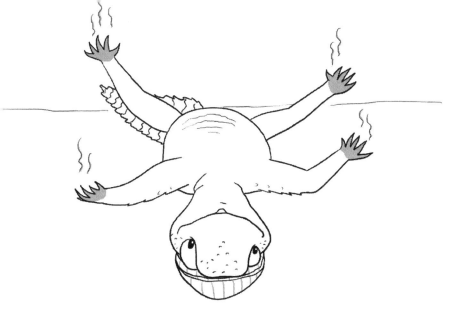

lizard.

The lizard turned on its back with its feet sticking up in the air. It looked so funny that Chee couldn't help laughing. Dae splashed some water from her box gently on to his red swollen feet.

"Ahhhh, that is so nice. Double Shukran!" the lizard said, his eyes rolling in his head again. Without warning, he closed his eyes and fell on his side.

Dae and Chee looked bewildered.

"Is he out cold?" Dae said.

"I don't know," Chee said, surprised. He gently poked him.

The lizard flew up in the air with a start and landed on his feet. He looked at Chee and said, "Double Shukran!"

Poor Chee had no idea what this lizard was saying.

Dae burst into laughter. "I think 'Shukran' is 'thank you' in Arabic," she whispered to Chee.

"You're so funny, Mr. Desert Lizard!"

"Me? I am not a desert lizard! I am Dhiz," he said.

"Well, you look like a lizard," Dae said.

"I do?" He looked strangely at himself, examining his feet and legs. "My mum said I am Dhiz when I was born. You can call me Dhiz the Liz!" A goofy grin spread across his face.

"So you are a lizard called 'Dhiz'?" Chee said.

"I am?" Dhiz said.

"You look like a lizard..." Chee started to say.

Dae put her flipper over Chee's mouth. "I think he's a bit crazy," she whispered.

"I am Dae and this is Chee," Dae said, pointing at Chee.

"You are so funny looking. Did you fall out of a tree and hurt yourself?" Dhiz said to Chee.

"No I did not! I am a chimpanzee," he exclaimed. "We all look like this!"

"A chimp who fell out of a tree and looks like you now," Dhiz said cheekily.

"Hey!" Chee said, "I am going to put you back in your sandbox if you're not careful!"

"No! Me super quiet now! Say no more!"
Dhiz said. At the same time he turned to Dae
and said, "Me like both you funny creatures
from afar. Did you fall from the stars? I see them
fall to Earth all the time. I ran many times to
catch them but the sand is so hot, so hot."

Dae stopped Chee as he was going to
lift Dhiz and throw him back in his sandbox.

"Where are you from Dhiz?" Dae asked
the lizard, who was now dancing. He stood
up on his hind legs and swayed his head back
and forth. It was a bizarre spectacle to behold!

"I am from Majlis Jinn," Dhiz said, spinning
around in circles.

Dae and Chee looked at each other,
thinking the same thing: he's mad. Dae burst
into giggles again – she had never seen such a
funny creature before.

Mad Dhiz the Liz, Chee thought.

"Next stop Meepa Tree. Hop off with me
and I'll show you my land," Dhiz said, jumping
up and down.

"Ooooh, how exciting – we should definitely go there Chee." Dae looked at Chee eagerly.

Chee leaned forward to whisper to Dae, "Yes, let's do that, but why don't we try and lose Dhiz. He is going to drive me crazy."

Dae smiled.

"Here it comes," Dhiz said. "Jump now!"

Chee and Dae jumped off the CP Train and landed on a white sandy beach. A sea of blue and green gently lapped the shore.

"Wow!" Chee and Dae said together.

"Aaaaah! We are here! We are here!" Dhiz was rolling and dancing about on the beach. He stopped when he careened head-first into a palm tree log!

"This is going to be a very funny and cra-zy adventure," Dae whispered to Chee.

"This way into the date plantation!" Dhiz was already running into a dense thicket of palm trees, rubbing his sore head.

Chapter 3
Wa-Wo Shoes

"Wait Dhiz! Dae can't walk on land!"

Chee called out to Dhiz, but he had already disappeared off into the thicket.

"We can take a Fafa," said Dae. "It's a motorbike with a sidecar. Look, they have one in that carriage!"

Chee looked where Dae was pointing. Sure enough, there was a motorbike, complete with a sidecar for a passenger.

"Wow! This is so cool!" Chee said, hopping on excitedly. Dae jumped into the sidecar, which just so happened to be filled with water.

"Step on it Chee!" Dae said gleefully. "Don't let Dhiz get away!" Chee started up the bike and zoomed off into the thicket.

It wasn't long before the pair caught up with Dhiz. The zany lizard was dancing between the rays of sunlight poking through the thick canopy of palm trees.

"Palm trees! We should stop and have some dates," Dae said.

Chee had never eaten dates and wanted to try some, now that he was on his big adventure. "I am great at climbing trees; I'll get them!"

Chee picked a tree with a wide trunk and rough surface, as it was the easiest to climb, and jumped on to it. As soon as he put his feet around the trunk however, all the rough bits smoothened and got slippery. "Eew! It's all slimy!" he said, sliding back down the trunk and landing with a thud on the ground.

Dhiz laughed, and then said, "Wa-Wo shoes! You need Wa-Wo shoes! That is the magical Meepa Tree, you can't climb the magical Meepa Tree without Wa-Wo shoes!"

Dhiz ran off deeper into the thicket, before Chee could even ask what he was talking about.   "He is crazy," he said to Dae, who had burst into a fit of giggles.

Dhiz was gone only a minute before returning with strange looking leaf-like balloons. "Wa-Wo shoes!" he declared, and started to wrap them around his feet. "Dae, blow into them!"

Dae's eyes widened and she gently blew air into each balloon. She couldn't help but giggle; Dhiz didn't really expect the Wa-Wo shoes to float, did he? But no sooner had she finished, Dhiz left the ground!

"Wooooo, off I go! This is the only way to get to the dates on the Meepa Tree!" Dhiz said, grabbing a low branch and swinging himself onto it.

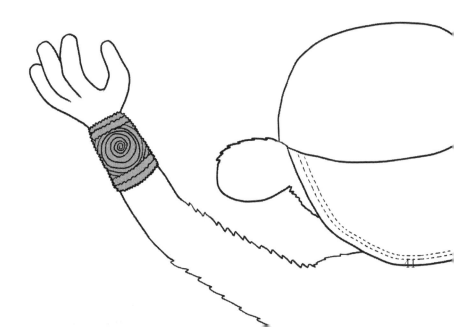

"Now your turn!" said Dhiz, removing the shoes. He let out the air and threw them down.

"What fun! I'm next!" Dae said, and tied the shoes to her tail while Chee blew into them. Up she went and nearly missed the branch, but Dhiz quickly grabbed on to her fin.

"How do we get Chee up now?" Dae asked. "There isn't enough room on the branch for all of us."

"Wait here!" Dhiz replied, before jumping higher up into the Meepa Tree. He returned momentarily clutching two dates: a plain blue one and a purple one with yellow spots.

"Eat the blue one Dae! It'll help you breathe out of water!"

Dae took the blue date from Dhiz and ate it; it tasted like chocolate.

"Look out below, Chee!" said Dhiz, throwing the purple date at him. Chee reacted too late as the date struck him on the head! "Ow!"

"Hurry up and eat it, before the spots turn green!"

"What?" Chee looked at the date and could see one spot already turning green. He quickly ate it, wondering what would happen to him.

Chee stood there for a few seconds. "Nothing is happening Dhizzzzz!" he squealed as he suddenly started floating upwards!

"It's working!" Dhiz shouted. "The purple date makes you float high enough to reach the top branch."

Chee tried his best to float towards Dhiz and Dae, but found it difficult. This wasn't anything like climbing a tree! Finally, he reached the top branch, but felt sick with all the swaying in the air.

"I didn't enjoy that," he said.

"Come on, no time to waste! Look for the Promga!" Dhiz said.

Dae's head was starting to spin with all these new names. "What does it look like Dhiz?" he asked.

"It's a large pomegranate, with multi-coloured jewels in it." Dhiz was shouting now as he skipped from one branch to another. The trunk was so huge, it was hard to see around it.

Dae saw Chee jumping onto another branch in the opposite direction to Dhiz. She looked at the Wa-Wo shoes. Hmmm, I am a bit wary of these shoes, better stay here till I get used to them, she thought to herself. I might pick a few extra blue dates just in case.

"Hey! I think I found the Promga!" Dae could hear an excited Chee shouting from somewhere around the tree.

A very excited Dhiz whizzed past her with super speed and grabbed Dae's flipper.

"Let me see, Chee!" Dhiz said, his eyes rolling in his head as he jumped up and down like a mad lizard. He nearly fell off the branch in his excitement.

Chee handed Dhiz the Promga. It was a large, jewel-encrusted pomegranate. One jewel was glowing brighter than the others, blue in colour and surrounded by a mist of stars.

"Key! Key! Key to the blue tunnel!" Dhiz said with joy, before clasping the jewel in his hand. "Now you guys grab it!"

Dae and Chee did the same. They waited a few seconds, but nothing seemed to happen. Dhiz looked confused for a moment, but then his face turned into a quirky smile. "We are supposed to twist and tap the jewel, like this!" he said while doing it.

No sooner had he done that, the Promga sprouted a large blue tunnel. The entrance was full of blue mist.

"Let's go before the tunnel disappears!" exclaimed Dhiz. "It's going to lead us to an exciting place. We can grab the Fafa as we go down."

The three entered the misty tunnel. Chee's heart was pounding with excitement.

Chapter 4
Sherf

Dhiz ran out into the blue misty tunnel. Chee sat on the Fafa and quickly drove it straight between the walls of the tunnels. The walls were starting to turn from mist to rock.

"Aaa, just in time," Dhiz said, trying to catch his breath.

"Why don't you climb into my seat?" Dae said as she hopped on the Fafa.

"Double Shukran!" Dhiz said.

"Look, the ground has turned into water," Chee said.

They all looked down to see the Fafa floating down a river.

"Wow, this is going to be a great adventure!" Chee said.

"Do you know where we are going, Dhiz?" Dae asked.

Dhiz shrugged his shoulders and said, "I don't know; I've never been in the blue tunnel."

It was very dark in the tunnel now. Suddenly, the tunnel was filled with fireflies. They clustered together and made a torch shape, lighting up the tunnel. Chee grabbed the torch and placed it on the handlebar of the Fafa; the fireflies glowed like a headlight.

"Brilliant idea, Chee," Dae said. "Look! The walls seem to be alive!"

Dhiz and Chee looked in the direction where Dae was pointing. The walls had many shapes, some like stars, turtles and funny looking plants, all changing shapes and colours constantly.

51

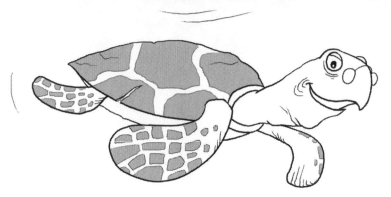

"Majlis Jinn…blue tunnel takes you to Majlis Jinn." A large turtle had just detached itself from the tunnel wall and was floating in front of them. "Majlis Jinn, beyond Wadi Naj," it said, smiling.

Dhiz leapt out of the Fafa and hugged the turtle. "I've heard so much about it – it has magic food! I want to go."

"Yes, that's true, and many more other magical things," said the turtle. "The Great Sul Haffah, the wise wizard, is going to be there. Beware though, the RaRa sisters are looking to create trouble and take over Majlis Jinn. They are capturing everyone and stealing their powers."

"That sounds dangerous. Are you sure it is safe to go to Majlis Jinn?" Dae said, her eyes wide open with concern.

"You cannot get there on your own. Wait, let me see if I can find Sherf," the turtle said.

He puckered his lips in a circle and blew out rings of blue mist. The rings bent and changed into misty turtles. They seemed alive, wispily swimming through the air, before dis-appearing into the tunnel walls in little puffs of blue smoke.

"I've sent the message through the mist; Sherf will be here soon," the turtle said.

"Sherf?" Dae asked.

53

"Yes, he is a turtle guide," replied the old turtle.

The water was starting to flow slightly faster, and its colour became an icy blue.

"Oooh, it's getting a bit cold," said Chee.

"Look inside your seat, there are some sweaters there," said Dae.

Chee opened the seat and pulled out three colourful sweaters. "Hmmm very strong colours Dae," he joked.

"What's life without colour?" Dae said, as she put on the purple sweater that Chee had thrown at her.

Dhiz looked funny in an oversized pink sweater. Dae was trying to fix it on him when they heard a weird bubbling sound. It was coming from the right side of the tunnel wall.

Blurp blurp blurp. The wall kept on making that noise. Then, a drenched turtle fell through it, nearly landing on Chee.

55

"Aah, here is Sherf!" said the old turtle, as his smile got bigger. "He will help you out from here. Good luck!"

The old turtle disappeared back into the wall. Just as his head was about to go in, he popped out again and shouted, "When Sherf can't hear well, blow hard in one ear to let the water out!"

"What?" Chee asked, but the old turtle had gone.

All three stared at Sherf. He had all kinds of sea animals attached to his body: starfish, oyster shells, even a seahorse around his waist. It was like he was a magnet for sea creatures! His eyes were filled with water and made him look as if he was crying.

Sherf beamed a wide grin; the poor turtle had several teeth missing. "Alloo!" he shouted.

"Allo?" Chee and Dae looked at each other, not sure what he was saying.

"Alloooooo!" Dhiz shouted back, before vigorously shaking Sherf's arm.

"Not so hard buddy! You'll pull my arm off!"

Dhiz laughed and shook Sherf's arm even harder, not realising the turtle wasn't joking. Of course he was more than shocked when he

pulled Sherf's arm clean off!

"Dhiz! What have you done?!" said Dae, shocked.

Dhiz looked worried, but Sherf appeared surprisingly calm. "Ooops," he said, matter-of-factly. "Starfish, could you reattach it?"

A tiny starfish peeled off from his shell and quickly stitched his arm back on with seaweed.

"Great, another crazy animal," Chee

whispered to Dae.

She laughed and said, "All part of the adventure! We can grow and learn so much from this."

"You're right, and it's fun too!" Chee said.

"*Ee avee oo cloum all o soof mouain.*" Sherf now sounded as if he was speaking underwater – none of the words made sense!

"Is it just me, but can anyone understand him?" Chee said.

"Ooooh, he must be talking a strange new language!" Dhiz said. "Oooo, aaaa, eeee."

"Stop! Dhiz!" Dae said. "What was it that the old turtle said before he left? Oh, yes!"

Dae blew hard into Sherf's ear; a stream of water poured out of his other ear.

"Ah, that's better!" Sherf said, sounding normal again. "My head fills up with water when I get too excited!"

Dae giggled – it was so funny.

"Now as I was saying, we have to climb Dune Mountain, to get to Wadi Naj." Sherf motioned them to follow him. He took out a starfish from his shell and put it to his ear. "Hi, starfish. We are here. Where are you?"

The starfish said, "I am here. Where are you?"

"Here, dear starfish," Sherf replied. "Good. Now that we all know where we are, let's go!"

Dae smiled at Chee. "Another crazy creature."

Chee nodded, stifling giggles.

"Here comes the opening to Dune Mountain," Sherf shouted.

Chapter 5
Wadi Naj

The opening for Dune Mountain looked too small to go through. Sherf didn't seem bothered by this as he walked towards it.

"Sherf won't fit through there," Chee said. But the opening grew wider as the turtle approached it. He stepped through and disappeared.

Dae looked at Chee. "Come on."

The opening widened further as Chee and Dae went through it on Fafa, with Dhiz clumsily following behind.

On the other side, Dune Mountain, a huge sand dune, loomed up in front of them. Sherf had already started climbing it, although he was making slow progress. His small feet sank into the soft sand and pulled him down-wards.

"This is going to take a long time, Sherf," Chee said.

"Why don't we put Dhiz's Wa-Wo shoes on the Fafa?" Dae suggested. "It might make it easier to drive on the soft sand!"

"Great idea Dae!" Chee said, taking the Wa-Wo shoes off Dhiz, who was now lying on his back with his feet up in the air.

"Now Dhiz, be careful!" warned Dae. "The sand will be very hot underfoot."

"Nonsense!" said Dhiz as Chee began attaching the Wa-Wo shoes to Fafa's tyres. The cheeky lizard leapt to his feet.

"Eeeh! Oooh! Hot! Hot! Hot!" Dhiz was screaming and jumping up and down, trying to keep his feet off the hot sand.

Dae and Chee burst into laughter as Sherf looked at Dhiz. "Is he all right?" he asked.

"I warned him about the hot sand!" Dae replied.

"Jump into the sidecar Dhiz," Chee said.

Dhiz jumped into the sidecar filled with water to cool his feet down. "Aah, much better! Double Shukran!" he said.

Sherf jumped into it as well, splashing water over Chee.

Dae laughed. "It wasn't me this time splashing water over you!" she said, climbing into the now crowded sidecar.

Chee smiled back and started up the

Fafa. The Wa-Wo shoes worked; the motor-bike progressed slowly but surely up the dune. "Wadi Naj is on the other side of Dune Mountain," Sherf said.

Just then, little glowing balls in different colours flew towards them. An orange one floated right in front of Dhiz. "Ooh, pretty!" he said, reaching out to grab it.

"No! Don't touch it!" Sherf shouted.

But it was too late. No sooner had Dhiz grabbed it, the orange ball turned bright red. The poor lizard tried to let go, but the ball was stuck fast and growing around him. Within moments, it had enveloped him.

"Nooo!" Dae watched in horror as the ball vanished into thin air; Dhiz was gone.

"Those are the RaRa sisters' Gobo Balls; they seek out and take anyone trying to get to Sul Haffah," Sherf said with a sad face. "Dhiz has been taken to somewhere in Majlis Jinn."

"We have to save him, Sherf," Dae said.

"Really? Can't we leave him there?" Chee joked, although Dae failed to see the funny side. "What do we do with all these other Gobo Balls?" he said, changing the subject.

"They can't harm you unless you touch them," Sherf said, looking down at his shell. "Now where is it? Starfish, go around my back and see if you can find it."

"Find what?" Dae asked.

"Ah, very good, starfish," he said as the starfish came back with a funny-looking coral. It was shaped like a cone, with a hole on one side. Sherf blew into the hole, creating a shrill whistling noise. Chee and Dae covered their ears.

The Gobo Balls flew towards the coral
and disappeared inside it. Sherf closed the
hole with another small coral. "*Owe y meii coo
u haaey,*" he garbled; there was water in his
head again.

"Ooh! My turn! My turn!" Chee said gleefully, before blowing into Sherf's ear. Water
streamed out of the other ear, like before.

"Thank you, Chee. As I was saying, the
trapped Gobos might come in handy," Sherf
said as he handed the coral back to the starfish. "Now let's go get your friend back!"

It was only a few minutes before they
reached the top of the dune. They could see
a beautiful place below them, filled with the
bluest of water. It was illuminated with light and
they could hear music and laughter.

"Wadi Naj," Sherf said with a smile. "It looks like the Naj festival is on. Yum yum, there will be great food!"

With all the excitement, Dae and Chee had forgotten how hungry they were. Their mouths watered at the mention of food.

"Tie that rope to the front of the Fafa – it will take us right into the centre of the Wadi."

Chee looked at where Sherf was pointing. The end of a long rope was dancing in front of them, jerking and motioning towards the Fafa. Chee noticed other strange cars and motorbikes around them, shaped like butterflies and dragonflies, each attached to their own ropes. They were being pulled down Dune Mountain, towards the Wadi.

Chee grabbed the rope and attached it to the Fafa; the rope went taut and began pulling them down, to the base of the dune, through the bustling festival, before finally stopping amidst a sea of floating bug cars.

Sherf jumped off and went running towards a food stand, which had popping seeds and seaweed of various colours. He ate a few

73

seeds, followed by some orange seaweed. "Try some," he said, offering seeds to Chee and Dae.

The seeds looked disgusting, but tasted delicious! Chee stuffed loads of them in his mouth. "I am starving," he said.

Dae put some in a little bag. "I am going to keep some for Dhiz; I'm sure he's starving too," she said with a sad face.

Chee hugged her. "We will find Dhiz, don't worry," he said.

"The Great Finfish will be able to help and guide us," Sherf said, looking around. "Let's

74

walk towards the water float – he is usually there telling stories to the children."

Chee and Dae followed him through the streets, which were filled with weird-looking creatures. Most of them looked like they had just come out of the water. There was a group of thin, tall fish on one corner singing, who sounded like they were still underwater. Everybody was happy, playing and dancing with their families and friends.

"Is that him?" Chee pointed to a large shark with many fins. He was dancing and singing to a large gathering of children.

Finfish turned his head and saw Sherf.

"Sherf, how good to see you again! And who are these lovely friends of yours?" he said as he motioned them all to come closer.

"OK kids, go and eat some of those delicious Tutom candies," he said, shooing all the young animals away.

Sherf introduced Chee and Dae to Finfish, who greeted them warmly. They spoke of the Hawa cave and the blue tunnel, of the magical Meepa Tree and the Promga. Finally, they spoke of Dhiz, their lost friend.

Finfish listened intently. "Your friend has been taken to Majlis Jinn," he said. "It is a long way away, across the dry desert. You'll have to take the Flying Jellies."

Chee didn't like the sound of Flying Jellies. "I don't like flying," he said. "I've already flown far too much today!"

"You've been so courageous so far Chee, and we have to save Dhiz," Dae said, putting her flipper on his shoulders. "He's our friend, and he needs us."

Chee took comfort in Dae's reassurance. She was right; he had done a lot of things which he never imagined that he would do, and it had taken a lot of courage. Saving Dhiz was just another adventure waiting to happen.

"Finfish, how do we get one of these Flying Jellies?" Chee asked, jumping up with new-found energy.

Sherf and Dae smiled.

"I have one coming here any moment; you are welcome to take it," Finfish said, motioning them to a large flat mushroom next to him.

"I'll get the Fafa!" Sherf said, running back to fetch the motorbike.

Chee and Dae sat down on the flat mushroom and looked around at the colourful Wadi. Through the crowd of colourful creatures, Dae saw Sherf driving the Fafa like a mad turtle towards them.

"Slow down, Sherf!" Dae shouted, but it was too late; he crashed into the mushroom, sending Chee and Dae flying!

"Oops! Sorry!" Sherf said, grinning.

"Here comes the Jelly," Finfish said, pointing to the sky. There was a huge pink jellyfish flying towards them. "Quick, grab its tentacles; it will only stop for a couple of minutes."

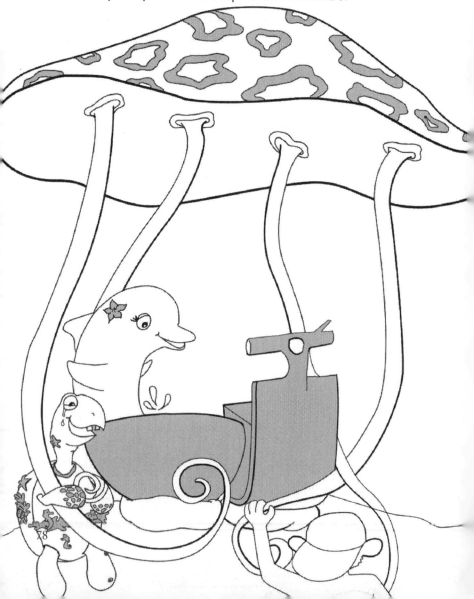

Chee and Sherf grabbed the tentacles and wrapped them around the Fafa. Dae and Sherf climbed into the sidecar as Chee got back behind the handlebar.

"Good luck finding your friend!" Finfish called out as the jellyfish lifted off and floated away. "Come and visit us again. I would love to tell you my stories."

"We will, Finfish. Thank you for all your help – you have been most kind," Dae said, looking down at him from above.

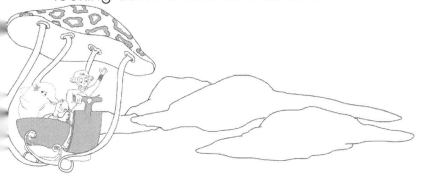

79

Chapter 6
Majlis Jinn

The Fafa, attached to the Flying Jelly, was drifting slowly away from Wadi Naj.

"It is so beautiful down there," Dae said. "Look! There is a white river flowing, with creatures drinking from it."

"That is the River of Juice," Sherf explained. "You close your eyes and think of your favourite juice, then take a sip; It'll taste exactly like that. Magical!"

"How wonderful!" Dae said, clapping. "I hope we can bring Dhiz here."

"We will. We are not far from Majlis Jinn. Keep an eye out for an old Myrrh Tree. There is a big hole close to it, which is the entrance to Majlis Jinn. You will smell the tree before you see it – it gives off a lovely fragrance," Sherf said.

Dae sighed with relief, knowing that they would soon be able to help Dhiz. She missed the crazy lizard.

"What's that coming towards us?" Chee was pointing behind Dae's shoulder.

Dae and Sherf turned to look where he was pointing. There were two dark shadows, floating towards them on what looked like dark orange rugs.

Sherf was almost falling off the Fafa to see the shadows more clearly. He jumped up in fright. "*Aaahee, ahhee, siiiiiiiis.*"

"Not now Sherf, speak properly," Chee said, blowing hard in Sherf's ear.

As the water spurted out of Sherf's ears, he shouted, "Ra...Ra...Ra...RaRa sisters!"

All three of them looked at each other, scared.

"They want to stop us from reaching Majlis Jinn!" Sherf continued. "They desire to seize it

from The Great Sul Haffah."

"Who is The Great Sul Haffah?" Dae enquired.

"No time to explain," Sherf replied. "I'll tell you later. First we have to stop the RaRa sisters."

"Maybe we can talk to them," Dae said optimistically. "Come to some sort of agreement."

Just then, a fireball flew past them, narrowly missing the Fafa. Sherf looked at Dae. "They're throwing fireballs at us Dae; I don't think they want to chat," he said.

"Fly faster, Jelly! We are in trouble, fly faster!" Chee was screaming to the Jelly.

Sherf spun round and presented his shell to Chee. "Quick Chee! Grab the Gobo Balls from my shell! They'll stop the fireballs!"

Chee grabbed a handful of Gobo Balls from Sherf's shell; the magical coral had made them safe to touch. Both of them started throwing the Gobo Balls at the fireballs, which froze them into balls of ice. They fell to

the ground and shattered, enraging the approaching RaRa sisters.

Chee suddenly had an idea to stop the sisters. "What if we took those flying rugs from under them?" he said.

"Yes! That could work!" Sherf exclaimed.

Chee readied himself as the sisters drew near. "We can't let you go to Majlis Jinn!" one of them shouted.

"You have our friend!" Dae shouted back. "Give him back to us!"

"We'll give him back if you promise never to return!"

Dae considered the sisters' proposal. Was it worth abandoning Majlis Jinn to them, just to get their friend back? She looked at Sherf, who was shaking his head. "We can't let them take Majlis Jinn," he said.

Dae had made up her mind. "Never! Majlis Jinn belongs to everyone!" she shouted with defiance. Chee and Sherf cheered with joy.

"Aaaaaaah!" The RaRa sisters were closer and angrier than ever before.

"We must work like a team," Chee said, taking charge. "On my signal, Dae, you lower the Jelly, Sherf, you grab the rug on the right and I'll go for the one on the left. Understand the plan?"

Both nodded.

The sisters were so close now.

"Wait, wait...NOW!" Chee shouted.

Dae pulled the Jelly down as Sherf and Chee leant over the sides of the Fafa. The first sister was caught by surprise as Chee whipped the rug from underneath her. She stumbled backwards and fell, but grabbed on to her sister's rug just in time.

"Sherf! Grab the other rug!" Chee cried out.

"I'm too short! I can't reach it!"

Chee watched as Sherf desperately tried to reach the rug. The little turtle leant further and further over; he was about to fall out of the Fafa!

Chee caught hold of Sherf's foot just in time, dangling the poor turtle over the side. Beneath him, the RaRa sisters were both now standing on a single rug. They appeared to be struggling for control; the one rug couldn't hold the two of them!

Chee then had another idea. "Dae! Let the Jelly fly higher now!"

Dae was confused. "But we're so close to the sisters!" she said.

"Trust me Dae!"

Dae did indeed trust her friend. She stopped pulling on the Jelly. It rose higher into

the sky, pulling the Fafa further away from the sisters.

"You can't catch us!" said Chee, trying to anger the RaRa sisters.

Chee's plan worked: the sisters were now fuming with rage. "You won't get away!" they said together.

The flying rug angled upwards in pursuit of the Jelly. It was then that the sisters realised why the chimpanzee was suddenly so keen to get away from them; it was a trick!

"I hope you two can stay on that rug!"

Chee called out.

The sisters screamed in terror as the unstable rug tilted back, throwing the pair of them backwards. They fought to stay on, but it was no use. A moment later, they'd both fallen off the rug, hitting the ground below in a cloud of black smoke.

"Yippee, we did it!" Sherf declared. All three jumped up and down with happiness.

"Do you think they are gone forever?" Dae said, looking down below.

"They know a lot of magic," Sherf said. "They'll be back, but hopefully not too soon."

The mood in the Fafa changed. Suddenly their victory against the RaRa sisters didn't seem like such a great achievement after all.

Sherf clapped his hands and changed the subject. "We must hurry and find the Myrrh Tree!" he said with excitement. "You'll probably smell it before you see it!"

"Hey, I smell something – it's like flowers," Chee said, sniffing the air.

"I can smell it too," said Sherf. "That's the Myrrh Tree! Take us down Dae!"

Dae pulled the Jelly down. As they descended, they saw a beautiful elegant tree in the middle of dry land.

"I don't see Majlis Jinn from here," said Chee.

"I think we have to follow the Myrrh scent on the ground and it reveals itself," said Sherf.

The Jelly landed close to the tree and they all unhooked the tentacles from the Fafa.

"Thank you, Jelly. Tell Finfish we are safe here when you see him next." Sherf kissed it goodbye.

The three watched in awe as the majestic Flying Jelly floated away.

Chee and Dae were looking at the Myrrh Tree; it was like a fairytale tree. It had long branches with lovely pink flowers. One of the branches was growing into the ground.

"I wonder if that branch is special?" Dae asked, although she could tell it was.

"Yes, come on!" Sherf was already running towards it as fast as his short turtle legs could carry him.

They stopped by the branch. Suddenly, the ground turned pink under them and gave

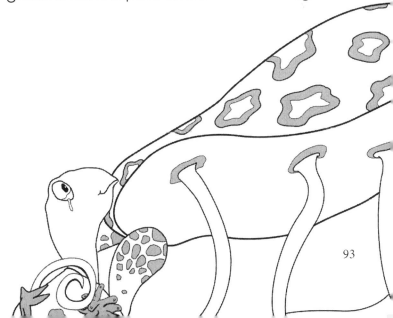

off the same lovely fragrance they had smelled earlier. Then, a set of pink footprints appeared in front of them.

"They smell so nice," Dae was saying as Chee drove the Fafa behind the pink footprints.

They must have driven for a few minutes when the footprints disappeared.

"Now what do we do?" Chee said.

They heard running footsteps behind them and a large fish ran past, jumped into the air and flew down in front of them. Just as he got close to the ground, it opened up and he disappeared into it.

"Hmm, not the weirdest thing I've seen today," said Chee, prompting laughter from Sherf and Dae.

"That must be the entrance to Majlis Jinn." Sherf was already running and off he flew into the air. Just like the fish before him, the ground swallowed him up.

Nervously, Chee and Dae turned the

Fafa around and did the same.

They fell into the hole that had opened up in the ground, and as they fell, the ground above closed again. It was very dark and they could not see where they were going. Instead of falling fast to the ground, they seemed to be floating gently down, as if warm air was carrying them from underneath. Chee and Dae looked at each other, both of them scared, both of them excited.

Suddenly, there were millions of fireflies flying all around them. The fireflies illuminated the walls around them, which were decorated

with depictions of ancient creatures. They all
seemed to be moving, as if trying to tell a story.
The movements were beautiful and hypnotic. It
was so quiet and peaceful.

Chee's eyes started to close, and he
said, "I can smell the scent of the Myrrh Tree
here."

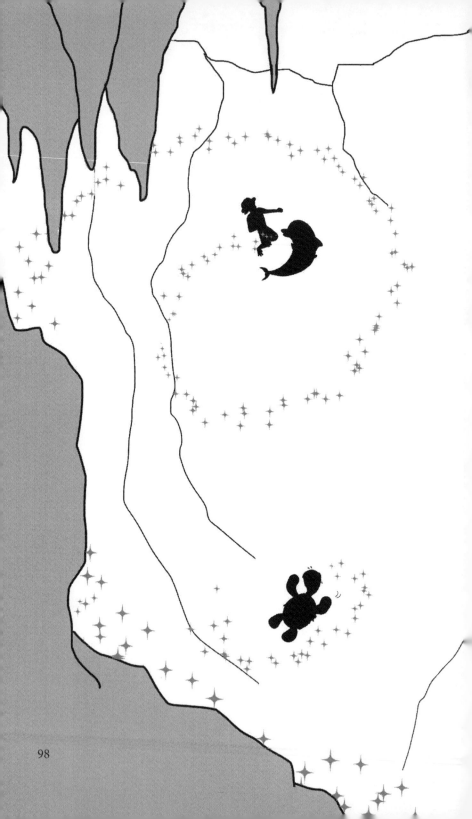

"Yes," Dae said. "What a beautiful fragrance. I think I might rest my eyes for a few minutes."

Soon Chee and Dae were both sound asleep, enjoying their well earned rest in the soft glow of the fireflies.

Chapter 7
The Great Sul Haffah

"Wake up! Wake up!" Sherf was shaking Chee and Dae. "We have to hurry and find Sul Haffah and warn him about the RaRa sisters."

Chee and Dae opened their eyes, as Sherf prepared Fafa.

"How long were we asleep?" Chee asked, feeling energetic. "I feel as if I've been asleep forever."

"No, actually just a few seconds!" Sherf said, much to Chee's disbelief. "You're in Majlis Jinn now, a land of pure magic! A second can be an eternity!"

Chee and Dae weren't sure what Sherf meant. Still, there was no denying the magic and wonder of their new surroundings.

Sherf and Dae jumped into the sidecar as Chee once again started up the motorbike. "Where to now?" he asked.

Sherf looked around confused – there were so many tunnel entrances to choose from. Sherf pointed to a tunnel with rain-bow-coloured stripes. "That way, I think," he said.

Dae didn't like Sherf's hesitance. "This is your first time here, isn't it?" she asked.

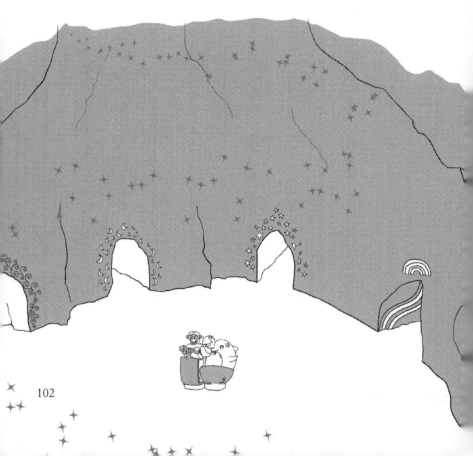

"Er, yeah," he confessed, "but they say in the land of magic, if you don't know what to do, follow the colours. That's what they say. I think..."

Chee turned the Fafa towards the tunnel and roared past the entrance. They must have driven a few seconds when the tunnel started to shake and turn. It felt like being in a milk-shake machine, like his mum had in her kitch-en.

"Aeeee, stop! I am going to be sick!" screamed poor Dae.

The tunnel stopped shaking just as a co-

lourful door opened in front of them.

"Ha! I was right!" Sherf squealed with glee. "Ladies and gentle monkeys, I give you: Majlis Jinn!"

Chee drove the Fafa through the door and into Majlis Jinn. They gasped in awe; the place was more spectacular and magical than they could have ever imagined. It looked like creatures and animals from all around the world were there. Some were huddled together talking, others were buying magical potions. Everything seemed to be on water.

"Are they walking on water, or is it a mirage?" Dae asked.

"It's magic Dae!" Sherf said with delight. "You can ask any question in Majlis Jinn, and the answer is always 'magic'!"

"Any question? Huh, better not ask where the bathroom is then," Chee whispered to Dae, who couldn't help but giggle.

Sherf hadn't overheard Chee. "Leave the Fafa here. We won't need it," he said.

The three of them dismounted the motor-bike as a strange creature approached. It was tall like a giraffe, had a thin neck like an ostrich and a small rabbit's head.

"Hey, it's a, Giraf-ost-rabbit!" Chee declared. Dae shook her head and laughed.

Sherf approached the creature. "Good day Sherf!" he said. "And who are these odd-looking creatures with you?"

Chee and Dae stopped laughing; who was he calling odd-looking?!

"Chohaha, these are my new friends Chee and Dae," Sherf explained. "We are looking for Wise Old Sul Haffah."

"Go straight over the square bridge – he is there telling his stories to all the young ones," Chohaha said.

"Thanks old friend! Come on, let's go."

Sherf had taken charge now and was forging ahead, with Chee and Dae following behind. Dae looked back at the funny creature. "What is Chohaha, Sherf?" she asked.

"Is the answer magic?" Chee asked sarcastically.

"No, but 'Chohaha' means 'hello' in magic," Sherf explained. "It can also mean goodbye."

"Aaah, so I was nearly right," said Chee. "'Chohaha'; I love how it sounds!"

Dae started to giggle; it was so funny.

They walked through the hustle and bustle of the street. It wasn't long before they came to a square bridge. It was a grand-looking bridge, like a giant platform, floating over the water. It had floating stones as steps. There were beautiful lanterns all around it. A strong mean-looking shark stood at the base of the steps with a long piece of wood in his fin.

"Stop! Who are you?" he demanded in a heavy voice.

Sherf looked scared and stood there silently.

Chee put his hand out and said, "Chohaha! We are here to talk to the great wise green turtle, Sul Haffah. It is about the RaRa sisters. Majlis Jinn is in danger."

The shark looked startled. "We have all heard about it. You must come quickly."

He jumped onto a stone step and told them to do the same. Once they were all standing on it, he swung his stick in the air. The steps started to fly over the bridge.

Dae looked back and saw a mist come over the entrance to the bridge, as if to block any more creatures from crossing it.

There were beautiful yellow and orange flowers on both sides of the bridge. The scent from them was soothing and enchanting.

As they approached the other side, they saw a large turtle sitting under a palm tree. There was deep sand around the tree and there were many baby creatures listening intently to the turtle.

"That must be The Great Sul Haffah," whispered Sherf, who had found his voice again.

The shark went over and whispered in The Great Sul Haffah's ear. Sul Haffah looked up at them, then smiled at the baby creatures around him and said in a deep husky voice, "Now, it's time to go home. I shall continue the story tomorrow."

"I want to hear the rest now Uncle Sul!" A baby turtle was clinging on to him and pleading.

"I know you do, my dear Haf. But it is late now and time for your bed."

Sul bid the children goodnight. They all ran and disappeared over the bridge.

"Thank you Qersh," Sul said to the shark. "I'll take it from here."

Qersh nodded and left the three friends in the presence of The Great Sul Haffah.

"Welcome – my friends," The Great Sul Haffah said to them. "Please come closer and sit by me."

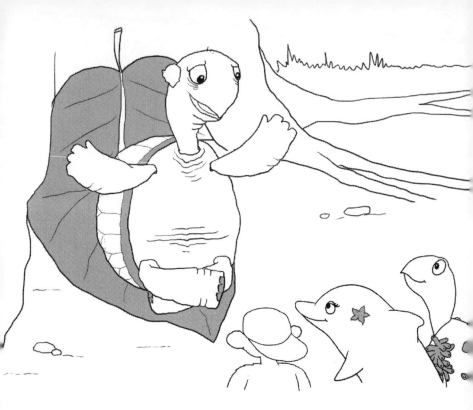

They all went over and sat around Sul, where previously the baby creatures had been sitting. Dae saw that Sul's shell was old, hard and green in colour. His eyes were full of wisdom and fun at the same time. Chee had never seen so many wrinkles on an animal before.

"You must be Dae," he said, looking at Dae, who looked back surprised.

"How did you know, Great Sul Haffah?" she asked.

"News travels fast my dear! And please,

call me Sul. That goes for you too Chee and Sherf."

"Sul, we have to tell you about the RaRa sisters. They—" Chee was interrupted by Sul.

"They have taken Dhiz and now are coming here to take over Majlis Jinn. I know all about it and how you tried to stop them. That was a very brave and clever idea Chee," Sul said. "They have survived the fall and are on their way here. I have many creatures keeping a watch to let me know when they come."

"Do you know where they have taken Dhiz?" Dae asked with concern.

"Yes, he is locked in the Aswad Cave, hidden deep within Majlis Jinn," Sul replied.

"How do we get there?" Chee asked.

"There is a yellow date with black crosses that grows on the Meepa Tree. Eating the date will transport you to the Aswad Cave. There's no other way into the cave, that I know of. Even the RaRa sisters don't know where it is."

Chee didn't recall seeing any dates like

that on the Meepa Tree. "What if the RaRa sisters took all the yellow dates?" he asked.

"Then you must find the cave by yourselves, but alas, I don't know where it is," Sul confessed. "The only clue is that an ancient plant called Sawa grows at its entrance."

"What does the plant look like Sul?" Chee asked.

Sul clapped and in a swirl of sand appeared a picture of a plant. They studied it closely.

Chee jumped up. "I know that plant!" he

said with excitement. "I saw it near the entrance to Majlis Jinn. It was deep inside a hole,
just above the ground."

"Then you must hurry! Go and save your
friend. We have been preparing special magic
potions and spells to stop the RaRa sisters. I'll
get my Green council to warn everyone in Majlis Jinn. Qersh, Qersh," Sul said, his voice getting
heavier.

Qersh appeared over the bridge.

"Take them to the entrance of Majlis Jinn,
and take the magical Bafa feather with you for
protection. Hurry, use the shortcut behind my

tree to get there." There was concern in Sul's voice, yet he spoke calmly.

They followed Qersh, who was already around the palm tree that Sul was sitting under. There was a huge door on the other side. Qersh took a small bottle and poured its contents in a hole to the side of the door. The water flowed quickly through the grooves in the door and finally stopped at the keyhole. Qersh pushed the door open and they all followed him.

"Please keep your hands and flippers inside the ride at all times," Qersh said with a cheeky grin. Suddenly, the ground underneath opened up and turned into a water slide.

"Ooooooh, this is so much fun!" Dae said. "It feels like the muddy slide in the estuary."

They swished and sloshed through the curving watery slide tunnel. They all landed in a pool of sparkling blue water. Dae looked down at the water; it was filled with magical sparkles. Chee ran his hand in the water and the magical dust followed his arm and hand. It was so

peaceful to be in the pool.

"This is The Great Sul's pool of magic. He comes over here to relax and think. It is a very sacred place. Only a few have seen it," Qersh said. "We must grab that rope on that corner and go across the stone wall of the cave."

"I can't do that," Sherf said with a sad face. "I can't climb walls."

"Come, get on my back. I'll carry you across – you too Dae," Qersh said, and helped Sherf get onto his strong back.

"He could probably carry all of us," Chee whispered to Dae, as he climbed across the wall without the rope. This was easy for him.

There was another door, and Qersh gently put Sherf and Dae down. He took another bottle of liquid out and poured it in a hole to the side of the door. Again, the liquid went in the grooves of the door and ended at the keyhole.

120

"It looks exactly the same as the previous door," Chee said.

"Yes, it is the ancient map of Majlis Jinn on both the doors. The Great Sul Haffah can find people through this map, with his magical powers," Qersh said as he pushed the door open and walked into a dark tunnel.

Chee whispered to Dae, "We're getting closer to Dhiz, I just know it."

Dae smiled back and nodded. The tunnel ahead was dark, but they could see a small light in front of them. Soon they came to the top of the tunnel.

"Wow, we're back at the entrance!" Chee said, looking out of the tunnel.

"It is a secret shortcut. Now Chee, do you remember where you saw the dark hole going to the Aswad Cave?" Qersh asked.

Chee looked around; there seemed to be more dark holes than he thought.

"Let's see now. When we landed, we were facing the rainbow tunnel, and I saw the

Sawa plant to the right. Over here!"

Chee scrambled quickly up the tunnel wall, before disappearing into a hole.

"He really is a very fast monkey," Sherf said, looking up at Chee as he went into one hole, and then another, and another.

They all waited patiently on the floor of the cave, and were just beginning to wonder if they would ever rescue Dhiz, when they heard Chee exclaim with great excitement: "I found it! I found it!" His head popped out from one of

the holes.

"How do we get up there?" Sherf asked. "It's too high for meeeeee—!"

Sherf didn't complete his sentence, as Qersh had picked him up and thrown him with a strong swift swing towards the opening of the hole.

"Get ready Dae, you're next. Don't worry, I'll be gentle," he said, looking at her worried face. After he swung her, he took a mighty leap and joined them.

"It's so dark in here; we need the firefly torches," Sherf said.

Chee and Qersh had already picked some from the side walls of the tunnel and gave one to Dae and Sherf. The tunnel lit up and the light from the torch cast all kinds of flickering shadows on the walls.

Sherf shivered in fear. "This is all so eerie and scary."

Dae put her flipper around him and said softly, "Stay close to me. It's going to be alright."

The tunnel widened, and there were many sand swirls in it. Most of them were empty, but some of them had creatures trapped in them.

"Look! There's Dhiz!!" Dae was pointing at a sand swirl in a far corner. Dhiz was trapped in the centre of it, in a trance.

Chee was about to reach into the sand swirl to save Dhiz, when Qersh pulled him back. "Don't, you will be sucked into it as well!" he warned. "It is a Ramal Dawama. We have to use the Bafa feather; it has many magical powers."

He took out the Bafa feather that Sul had given him and started to swirl it around the Ramal Dawama. The sand swirl started to slow down and fall to the ground. When it got to Dhiz's feet, the sleeping lizard slowly opened his eyes. "Double Shukran," he said sleepily.

Dae grabbed Dhiz and hugged him. "Dhiz! You're alright! You're alright!"

"Of course I'm alright!" Dhiz said, unaware of his ordeal. "I just fell asleep, that's all. Where are the lovely glowing orange balls?"

"The Gobo Balls! You weren't supposed to touch them. That is why you are here in the Aswad cave," said Qersh.

"Ooooh, hello new friend!" Dhiz said, shaking Qersh's fin up and down like mad. Chee and Dae laughed, although Qersh wasn't amused.

"Come on, we have to get back to The Great Sul!" Qersh said, yanking his fin away from Dhiz. "The RaRa sisters could return at any time."

"You know Sul? Tell me more! Please! Please! Pretty please!" Dhiz was rolling his eyes and jumping up and down in excitement.

"I'll fill you in on the way Dhiz, but for now we must hurry," Dae said as she saw Qersh run-

ning towards the entrance of the cave. "Oh I almost forgot, I have something for you to eat!" Dae gave Dhiz the Tutom candies, which he greedily gobbled up.

Qersh had run far ahead, but the rest of the gang weren't far behind. He was at the mouth of the cave when he stopped them all suddenly. "Shh!" he said, pointing down at the bottom of the Majlis Jinn cave.

It was the RaRa sisters! They had returned, now both riding on a large carpet. They had brought several glowing boxes with them.

"Those boxes contain stolen magic," Qersh whispered. "We have to warn Great Sul; Majlis Jinn could be in danger!"

Qersh led everyone back into the Aswad Cave, away from the evil sisters. The only way out now was back up the water slide.

Chee and Qersh searched around for the slide. Dae meanwhile was mesmerised by the poor animals still trapped in the swirling sands. "Could you not set them free Qersh?" she asked. "Perhaps one of them could help us out."

Qersh liked Dae's idea and started circling the Bafa feather around the swirls. One by one the animals came out of their deep sleeps. There were birds, mountain cats and a tiny little turtle.

"Now to find a way from this cave to the water slide," Chee said, looking around for something that might help them.

The baby turtle tugged on Chee's leg and spoke in a soft slow voice, "The water slide to Uncle Sul's tree?"

"Yes!" they all said, and startled the poor baby turtle.

"I know where it is. I was playing on it and got lost and ended up here. Then I tried to touch the big cat there through the sand and got myself trapped. I want to go home," said the turtle as a tear rolled down his cheek.

Chee knelt down to speak to him. "You have to be very brave now and help us get out of this cave," he said. "Majlis Jinn is in great danger and we need to get to your Uncle Sul as soon as possible."

Dae looked at Chee; she was so proud as to how he was handling the baby turtle.

"I am Fah. I'll help you," the baby turtle said, wiping his tears.

Fah spoke of a hole towards the back of the cave, which led straight to the magic pool. Qersh picked him up and put him on his back and asked him to take them to the hole.

They found the hole and Qersh jumped in first, followed by Dae, Dhiz, Chee and then lastly Sherf. It was a muddy slide and it turned right and then left sharply, sending them into a spin! The crazy slide ended at the magic pool,

which they landed in with a great splash. Dhiz crashed into Sherf, who was spluttering in the water.

"*Geee ooooouf eeeeee!*"

Poor Sherf! His head was clogged up with water again. "There there, poor turtle. Me help you," Dhiz said, vigorously shaking Sherf's head!

"*Noooooooottttt liiiiiike thaaaaaat!*" Sherf screamed. But the water did stream out of his ears and he was soon back to normal.

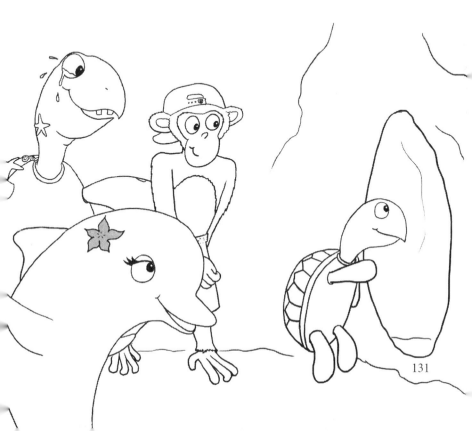

"You're welcome!" Dhiz said, misreading Sherf's angry stare.

"Stop fooling around you two," Qersh said. "We need to find a way up the slide – it's too slippery for anyone to go back up."

"There's a rope at the top of the slide; we can use that," Fah said.

"I can do this," Chee said to Qersh. "If you throw me up there, I can get the rope."

Qersh thought for a moment, and then nodded his head.

They all went to the back of the pool, where Dhiz was playing with the magic dust in the water. Qersh picked up Chee and threw him up the slide.

Chee clung to the water slide and started to climb up. He was soon at the top and saw the thick rope. One end was tied to a large hook on the wall; he picked up the other end and threw it down. "Here it comes!" he shouted down the slide.

It wasn't long before Dae came up, followed by Dhiz. Qersh was the last up, with Sherf and Fah on his back.

They returned to the door they'd previously come through. Qersh once again took out a bottle of liquid and poured it into the tiny hole on the side. Soon the door opened and they were outside the big palm tree.

As they ran around it, they saw Sul, with more turtles sitting in front of him, talking. They

all stopped and turned to look at Qersh and the others.

"Fah! My dear Fah! You are safe! We've all been so worried about you." Fah had jumped from Qersh's back and was in Sul's embrace. "Now, now, don't worry. You must be tired and hungry and I know your mother is worried sick. Go home with Uncle Bren."

A large turtle walked towards Fah and took him away.

"Chohaha, Chee!" Fah said, waving to everyone.

Chee smiled at him and waved back. "Chohaha, my little brave friend."

Chapter 8
Zardar

"Great Sul, the RaRa sisters have entered Majlis Jinn," Qersh said.

Sul had been joined by a group of ancient green turtles, who all appeared concerned with Qersh's warning.

"It is time," Sul said with a serious face. "Qersh, go to the bridge and gather all your strongest marine animals and tell them to guard each of the tunnel entrances."

Qersh was already on his way. Sul turned to look at Chee and the gang. "I see that you found your friend Dhiz. Please tell me all that you saw in detail."

They told him about their little adventure, the water-slide, the Ramal Dawama swirls and the animals trapped within them. Finally they spoke of the RaRa sisters.

"The sisters had many glowing boxes full of magic potions with them," Dae said.

"They have stolen magic from all over Majlis Jinn," Sul said, looking at their worried faces. "I have gathered all the ancient council members here, who each have a magical gift. We are going to combine all our efforts to stop them."

Sul clapped and muttered a magical phrase. Then, a screen of sand rose out of the ground. It looked like a television screen. It showed the front of the bridge, and they could see Qersh standing there talking urgently to two other sharks.

"Dhiz, keep an eye on this. Let me know if you see the RaRa sisters."

"Yesss, I'll keep both eyes on it," Dhiz said, rolling his eyes round and round. Chee and Dae looked at each other, wondering whether it was a good idea to let him keep guard, but

they would not dare question Sul's authority.

"Now, my great Green council, place your magic in this clay tray," Sul said, pointing to a large tray, which had a large open bowl in the middle, surrounded by small bowls. There were thin grooves running from each of the smaller bowls to the big one.

Each green turtle came over and started placing their magic potions in a bowl. Soon all the bowls were full with different magic. Some looked like liquid, some small stones and others like powder.

"Now for the ZarZar liquid," Sul said, taking out a small green glass bottle. He opened the bottle and poured out its liquid into the middle bowl. "It will take a few minutes before all the other magic potions mix to make the Great Zardar powder ball."

"Look, the RaRa sisters!"

Everyone turned to see Dhiz pointing and shouting at the sand screen; the RaRa sisters were on it. They had made it inside Majlis Jinn and were throwing black powder everywhere, which turned the inhabitants of the cave into misty sand statues.

141

"Oh, no, the poor creatures," Dae said, her eyes widening with worry.

"The sisters have become more powerful. Quick, my great Green council, go and help Qersh guard the bridge entrance. Chee go with them, use your wit and agility like you did to fight them near Wadi Naj," Sul said.

Chee ran with them, eager to help.

"Dhiz, you have done well. Could you do another job for us? It is very important," Sul asked.

Dhiz nodded, jumping up and down. He was never given any responsibility, and he felt so happy to be able to help.

"Let me know when the Zardar powder ball takes form," Sul said.

Dae smiled at Dhiz, pleased for him. She went and sat beside Sul, watching the sand screen intently.

Sul looked at her and gently said, "We will be fine. Just stay close to me, dear Dae."

Dae nodded.

The RaRa sisters were moving through Majlis Jinn very quickly, turning everyone they encountered into sand statues. Soon they were close to the entrance of the bridge.

Sul and Dae stood up, watching with concern. They saw Qersh throwing white light through his stick at the RaRa sisters. They had created dark mist monsters that were fighting for them against the Majlis Jinn Green army.

At the same time, Chee went for the magic boxes on the carpet. Qersh shouted at him, "Open them, throw them at the RaRa sisters and shout 'MaJi'."

Chee quickly did as Qersh said. As soon as he threw the contents of the box on the RaRa sisters and said "MaJi", the RaRa sisters screamed. They slowed down for a few seconds.

"Keep doing it, Chee – it's working," Qersh shouted.

Chee grabbed another box and did the same. This time one of the RaRa sisters moved away, so that the magic didn't fall on her. She went for Chee and grabbed his ankles. "You! I will turn you to sand!" she said, and threw the black powder at him.

Qersh jumped in front of Chee to protect him. Sul and Dae watched in horror as the black powder fell on him and he turned into a sand statue.

Chee shouted, "Nooooo," and threw lots of magic boxes at the same time at the RaRa sister, shouting "MaJiiii". She turned a horrible green colour and froze.

"Chee has only a few minutes before she

turns back," Sul said to Dae.

The other sister had turned to Chee. With an awful scream, she picked up a Gobo Ball with a black glow and threw it at Chee. It was so sudden that Chee didn't have time to move away and the Gobo Ball hit him on the back. Dae and Dhiz had tears in their eyes as they watched Chee's body turn slowly into a black mist.

"Sul!" Dae looked at him, her eyes begging for help.

"I can't help him at the moment Dae. Dhiz, has the Zardar powder started to take shape?"

Dhiz looked inside the magic bowl. "It's starting! I can see half the ball!"

"We need a few more minutes," Sul said.

The green turtles were defending the entrance to the bridge as best as they could, but the green spell on the other RaRa sister had ended and she was angrier than before. Both the RaRa sisters threw Gobo Balls at the turtles and, one by one, they all turned to that awful black mist.

The bridge was unprotected. The RaRa sisters jumped on the carpet and flew over the bridge. Dae and Dhiz hid behind Sul in fear.

The RaRa sisters were soon standing in front of Sul. "The Great Sul! Look at you, unprotected, vulnerable. First we'll take you, then we'll take Majlis Jinn and rule the world of magic forever!"

The sisters laughed maniacally. They picked up their largest Gobo Ball and flung it at Sul. Sul stared at them calmly, before clapping his hands together with a loud bang. "ENOUGH!" he shouted.

Sul had unleashed his most powerful magic, creating a sandstorm that flew all around the sisters. Their magic couldn't penetrate the storm; each Gobo Ball they threw crashed into the sand and disappeared. But Dae could see that each time they hit the sandstorm with magic, it got weaker.

"It's not going to hold much longer," she whispered.

Sul nodded and looked at the magic bowl; the Zardar ball was nearly done.

The RaRa sisters meanwhile had opened up a black box decorated with bones and removed a pulsating black ball; they'd saved their strongest magic for this occasion. Both threw it with their might at the sandstorm. Dae watched in horror as the dark magic shattered the storm.

The RaRa sisters threw their heads back and laughed. "Now Sul, you have lost everything!" they shouted as they flew towards Sul.

They were only a few metres away when Sul bent down and picked up the completed Zardar ball and threw it at the sisters. They saw it coming towards them in horror and their eyes widened with fear. They tried to stop and turn away, but it was too late. The Zardar ball hit them with a loud swish and turned into high wind. It circled around them from head to toe. Both the sisters were suspended within the Zardar wind. All their magic was gone and they were like pieces of broken branches hanging in midair.

"RaRa," Sul said in his loud voice, "you have been given many chances to change your ways to good. But you have always chosen the path to hurt others and control them. You cannot be part of a community. I am banishing you to the Yajaf Sahara, with no magic powers. There you will have to submit to the power of nature to survive. You are not to return here till you have learnt to live in peace."

There was anger and fear in the RaRa sisters' eyes.

"ZarZar, akhaj, akhaj te Yajaf Sahara, yalla!" Sul declared.

The Zardar wind started to circle faster and faster, blowing the sisters around like a cyclone. It disappeared with a loud bang; the RaRa sisters were gone.

"I open eye? I open eye?" Dhiz said. He had covered his eyes and had been shaking like a leaf behind Sul.

"Yes, it's over Dhiz, you are safe," Sul said.

"Look!" Dae exclaimed.

All the creatures in Majlis Jinn were coming back to life – the black mist was disappearing.

Dae saw Chee and ran over the bridge and hugged him tightly. "You were so brave, Chee. I am so proud of you!"

Chee grinned back. "It was all a team effort," he said, and walked towards Qersh. "Thank you, Qersh. I shall never forget what you did for me."

"No, thank you, dear Chee and Dae, for helping us save Majlis Jinn."

Sul had walked over the bridge. All the creatures turned and stood in awe of Sul. "Dhiz and Sherf, you have been of great service to your land." He took out two corals from his shell and gave one to each of them. "These magic

corals will take you anywhere in this beautiful land."

"Double Shukran!" Dhiz was jumping up and down with excitement.

Sul roared with laughter. "'Double Shukran'? Haha, you might be starting a new trend in saying 'thank you', our crazy lizard friend."

He turned and looked at Chee and Dae. "This is an ancient Nubian stone. It carries the history of our land. Ask a question and it will reveal all. Use it well," Sul said as he put a necklace each over their heads. They were beautiful – shiny shades of brown stone.

"Thank you Sul," Dae said, hugging him.

"You mean 'Double Shukran'," he said with a wink.

Everyone burst out laughing. Dhiz was grinning and jumping up and down with happiness.

"Sul, I have to get back to the estuary now. My mum will be waiting. Is there a quick way of getting to the CP Train?" Chee said.

"My dear Chee, there is always a quick way with magic. Stand back," Sul said, rubbing his feet together and creating a green dust.

"Wait. Dhiz, are you coming with us?" Dae said.

"I want to stay here. Me like here," he said, and ran over to give them hugs. "Come soon!" he said, licking Chee's face.

"Eew...stop!" Chee said, laughing. "We will, Dhiz. Look after yourself."

"Bye Sherf, Qersh, great Green turtles, Sul," Dae said as the green dust started whirling around her and Chee.

"Wait!" Chee shouted. "The Fafa!"

Just then, Chohaha appeared on the motorbike. The poor animal could barely fit on it, his legs dangling in the sidecar. Everyone roared with laughter as he clumsily climbed out of it. "You left this behind!" he said, laughing too.

Chee and Dae climbed into the Fafa and waved to everyone. The green dust

whirled so fast that they couldn't see anything; it stopped swirling suddenly and disappeared. They were back on the beach and could hear the CP Train in the distance.

"Quick, let's get into it," Dae said. "It looks like it's going back to Fizz."

"It'll be nice to see home again, but I'm going to miss Majlis Jinn," said Chee.

"Majlis Jinn?" a creature that looked like a hippopotamus asked them from the next carriage. "What's it like?"

Chee and Dae looked at each other and smiled.

"Magic!" Chee said.

"Tell me more!" the hippo said.

They told the hippo the whole adventure, and were at the end when the CP Train stopped at the estuary.

"We have to get off here, hippo. Chohaha, as they say in the magic world," Dae said.

They jumped off, with Chee on Dae's back. Dae gently swam to the beach and

Chee hopped off her back. He turned and gave her a huge hug. "Thank you for showing me Majlis Jinn – it was magical."

"You mean 'Double Shukran'?" Dae said, grinning. "It was so much fun. You must go now – your mother might be worried. Will I see you again? Maybe we can go for another adventure?" Dae continued, splashing water at him.

"Haha! Try and keep me away! By-eeeee."

Chee was already running through the tunnel. He thought about his whole adventure as he ran back home.

Till the next magical adventure!

Glossary

Chee
The cheeky chimp

Dae
The daisy dolphin

Dhiz the Liz
The crazy desert lizard

Sherf
The green turtle with wa-
ter-clogged eyes

Sul Haffah
The great wise turlte

Qersh
The strong shark guard

Glossary

The RaRa Sisters
Made of black dust who fly
on magic carpets

Finfish
The wise storytelling shark

Haf
The baby green turtle

Fah
Haf's twin brother

Zarfe
The shy giraffe

Hippo
The bubbly hippo

Glossary

CP Train
The centipede train which takes you to magical places

Fafa
Motorbike with sidecar

Meepa Tree
The magical tree with magical coloured dates

Meepa Dates
Full of magical surprises

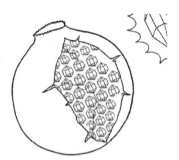

Promga
The pomegranate with the magical jewels

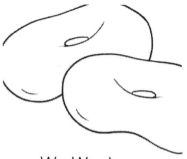

Wa-Wo shoes
Leaf balloons which help you fly

Glossary

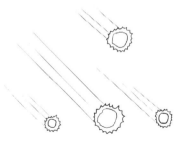

Dune Mountain
Mountain of soft sinking sands

Gobos
RaRa sisters use these to capture you

Tutom Candies
Candies that pop in your mouth with your favourite flavour

Flying Jelly
Takes Fafa to Majlis Jinn

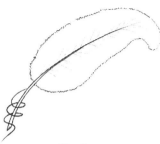

Bafa
Sul Haffah's magical feather

Ramal Dawama
Black swirling magical dust that puts one in a trance

Glossary

ZarZar liquid
Sul Haffah's magical potion

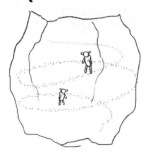

Aswad Cave
The black cave

Zardar Ball
The most powerful magic made from all the Green Council's magic

Nubian
Full of magical surprises

MaJi
Shout it with magic and it slows the RaRa sisters

Chohaha
Hello and Goodbye

Double Shukran
Dhiz's way of saying thank you

This is Saniya Chughtai's first book in the series "The Adventures of Chee and Dae"

Saniya Chughtai is the founder of the edutainment brand The Wadi Tribe. She is also an avid author of children's stories, a love which began when listening to her father telling stories in her native land, Pakistan. This passion was fanned by years in Ireland, her new homeland, listening to the many Celtic myths. This latest series is a story about two unlikely friends, a chimp and a dolphin known as Cheeky Chimp and Daisy Dolphin, or Chee and Dae to their friends.

So come and join these two adventurous souls as they traverse the fantasy world in search of fun, friendship and adventure!

"Lots of Love, Light, Truth and Energy to all"
Saniya

Made in the USA
Columbia, SC
21 June 2020